# Behind the Door

by

## Paul Kropp

LIBRARY AND ARCHIVES CANADA CATALOGUING IN PUBLICATION

Kropp, Paul, 1948–
    Behind the door / Paul Kropp.

(HIP edge)
ISBN 978-1-897039-26-7

    I. Title.  II. Series.

PS8571.R772B43 2008      jC813'.54      C2007-906932-0

General editor: Paul Kropp
Text design: Laura Brady
Illustrations drawn by: Catherine Doherty
Cover design: Robert Corrigan


    2 3 4 5 6 7      15 14 13 12 11


Printed and bound in Canada

High Interest Publishing acknowledges the financial support of the
Government of Canada through the Canada Book Fund for our
publishing activities.

Jamal and his buddies like to hang out
in the basement of an old warehouse.
Everything is fine until a strange door
appears on an inside wall. Of course,
the guys have to look behind that door —
and then the horror begins.

Dedicated to Algernon Blackwood, who wrote the best ghost stories ever. And to my sister, who actually saw a ghost in our basement.

— PAUL KROPP

# CHAPTER ONE

The Door

*They were all coming at me.* *I could see them, floating in the air. They had bodies but no bodies, faces but no faces. The ghouls floated up over me, their teeth shining white in the dark.*

*Then I heard a voice from somewhere over my head. "We want you, too, Jamal. Your friends are with us. Now we want you."*

*I screamed. I ran back to the exit door, trying to get out, but it didn't work. There was* no handle, and there was nothing to hold onto. The door didn't budge.

And then I got freezing cold, just like the basement all around me.

The ghouls came closer. I could see their breath, white in the air. I could see their teeth, their sharp pointy teeth, getting closer to me. I pulled back. I tried to put one arm up to hold them back, but it was hopeless. I was trapped against the door. The ghouls kept coming at me. It was dark, pitch dark, and all I could see was their teeth.

"Gotcha," Amos shouted, and that made us all jump.

"Not a bad story, Jamal," Delmar added. "What's gonna happen next? The ghouls get your face, or what?"

"Nah, Jamal's face is too ugly," Amos said. "No ghoul wants to eat a face like that. They'll want a real nice face, like mine."

We all laughed. Amos was like that, bragging about nothing.

"Ghouls or girls?" Delmar asked him. "Far as I can see, there ain't no girls going after your face, Amos. So maybe it's a face only a ghoul could love."

We laughed again. The three of us made fun of each other a lot. We'd been friends since forever. Okay, so maybe not that long. But we'd been friends since Delmar moved to the Edge and started to hang with Amos and me.

Amos is the smart one. He gets all the good marks and aces all the math tests. I'm pretty good at writing stories, but Amos is good at *everything*.

Of course, Amos is funny looking. He's got a big, wide nose and these little square glasses that sit on it. He looks like that kid on *Family Matters*, Steve Urkel. I used to tell guys that I hung out with a TV star.

Then there's Delmar. You put the accent on the end of his name, like Del-MAR. He can play just about any sport there is. His favorite is basketball, maybe because he's tall and skinny. He wants to play football, too, but his ma won't let him.

Then there's me — Jamal. I'm not really that ugly, but girls don't look at me much. I'm not like Delmar. I don't have to fight the girls off the way he does. And I'm not smart like Amos. I'm kind of in-between. Not that smart, not that dumb. But I got a pretty good brain when it comes to stories. Maybe I'll be a writer like that Walter Dean Myers guy. You never know.

The three of us got a lot in common. I mean, we *have* a lot in common. We don't have any money and we don't have any dads to bug us at home. Amos never had a dad. Delmar's dad took off before he moved here. And my dad's in jail. Cops caught him dealing and sent him off for seven years.

My mom says I'm gonna turn out just like him. Thanks, Ma.

The three of us hang out in a space under this old warehouse. Delmar found the place. We were playing basketball at the rec center, and some guys

started to hassle us. The three of us, we're not fighters, so we took off. We ran to where all the warehouses are. Then Delmar jumped down these stairs. Amos and I piled in after him. The guys who were after us went right on past, but we stayed down there.

Amos started playing with the door in front of us. It was one of those push-button locks. You hit the buttons the right way, the door unlocks. There's maybe one chance in a million that you get the numbers right, but Amos got it — second try.

So the door swung open to this basement. There wasn't much in there, just a big room under a warehouse. The walls were made of concrete blocks. There were two little windows to let in some light. The floor was concrete, with broken concrete blocks and bricks at the edge. Like I say, it wasn't much.

But we kind of fixed the place up. First we swept off some of the floor near the door. Then we found some busted chairs and an old table to bring down.

Delmar came up with an old rug on garbage day. I got an extra lamp from my grandma's place and we found a way to wire it up. It didn't look half bad when we were done. Really.

Delmar said the basement was our clubhouse. Okay, it wasn't like the country clubhouse that the rich kids have up near the park. But it was ours. We had found it and made it our own. Nobody else ever came down there.

Okay, we sometimes brought a little brother down. But we made him wear a blindfold to keep it secret. I mean, what good is a clubhouse if it's not a secret? That's what makes it cool.

So we were down in the clubhouse when I read my story. Well, the start of my story, 'cuz I still had 500 words to go. I had to write it for Mr. Donkey, our English teacher. (Okay, his real name is Mr. Donkas, but who cares?) We only had one light down there, so that's where I was. Delmar, he sat on the chair. Amos was lying on this old bed.

It was Delmar who saw the door.

"What's that?" he said. (It came out sounding like *whazzat?*)

Amos and me looked over. All three of us looked at the back wall of the basement. We'd been looking at that wall for a year — and there was nothing. I swear, there was nothing.

But now there was a door.

"Somebody put in a door," Amos said. Like I said, he's the smart guy.

"Yeah, since yesterday?" Delmar said. "You can't put in a door in one day."

"Sure you can," I told him. "Door guys, they're real fast."

"What do you know about door guys?" Delmar said.

"More like doorknobs," Amos threw in. "Jamal knows all about doorknobs — 'cause he's kind of a doorknob himself." And then both of them laughed.

So I shut up. Those two love to give me a hard time, like they're oh-so smart and I'm oh-so dumb.

"C'mon," Delmar said. "Let's check it out."

We only had one flashlight, so it was hard to see much. The three of us walked to the back wall and shone the light on the door. It was a green metal door with rust down at the bottom. The door had two long metal pieces that made an X, and bolts to hold those on. It looked like the door to an old bank vault. Or the kind of door you'd see on an old ship.

"Don't look like a new door to me," Delmar said. "Looks like a real old door."

"Except we've never seen it before," Amos added. "Like, ever."

Then we had one of those moments. It was like the *Twilight Zone*. There should have been music, or something. Instead we just heard this rumble from over our heads. The guys in the warehouse were moving something. They were moving stuff, and we were frozen.

Now me, I wasn't scared. The other guys, maybe they were scared, but not me. I don't get scared, except when Mr. Donkey gives us a grammar test.

But I had this funny feeling. I felt like there was

something really *wrong* about this door. Like it didn't make sense. It just wasn't kosher — that's a word my buddy Jake uses. It was weird.

"So you open it," Delmar said.

"Not me," I told him. "There might be rats back there. You know how I feel about rats. How about you, Amos? You open it."

"Why should I?" Amos snapped. "The flashlight's almost dead. We won't be able to see anything anyhow. What's the point?"

"You're scared," I said.

"Yeah, kind of," Amos admitted. "You want to make something of it?"

"You ain't scared of me," I told him. "You're scared of a door — a stupid door."

"So you open it," he said.

"No problem, man," I told him. Then I reached out and grabbed the handle. It was cold, real cold. I mean, the basement was always kind of cold, but this was real cold.

I tried to turn the handle. "It's locked," I said.

"Told you," Amos said.

"Did not," I snapped back.

And then we all started yapping and joking, just like the door wasn't there. It's no big deal, I told myself. The guys who own the warehouse, they put up a door. It's simple. It might seem a little weird, but it's simple.

Dead simple.

# CHAPTER TWO

Breakthrough

"Where you been?"

That was my mother. She never says, "Nice to see you, Jamal." Never "How'd you like school today?" Just the old question — Where you been?

"With the guys," I said.

"What about your homework?"

"Later," I told her.

"Later!" she shouts back. "Always later. When you gonna smarten up, Jamal? The way you're going, you're gonna end up like your daddy. School's the only chance you got, boy."

"Right, Ma."

"You hanging out at that warehouse again? Don't tell me no. I can see it on your dumb face. I tell you, Jamal, you better get straight right now. Homework first, hanging later. Nobody ever got to college by hanging — you hear what I'm saying?"

Sure I heard her. My mom's been saying the same thing for the last sixteen years. Maybe she even told me before I was born, but I didn't hear so well back then.

I don't explain much to her anymore. I could have told her that I was trying out my story. I could have said that the guys were helping me. I could have told her about Mr. Donkey and all that — but why? Some parents just don't listen. Some parents just give you lip.

So I did my homework. Like, I almost got the story done. I was working on it when my little brother came in.

"What you writing, Jamal?" he asked.

"A story," I told him.

"Read me," he said.

"I can't," I told him. "It's too scary. You'll have nightmares. You bring me one of your books. You're too little to hear about ghouls."

"What's a ghoul?"

"A thing," I said. "A bad thing."

"Like Mr. Donkey?" I had told Shaq all about Mr. Donkey.

"Nah, worse than Mr. Donkey. A ghoul is a thing that will eat your face — just like this." Then I used my hand and sort of mushed his face.

My little brother just laughed, and then I read him a storybook.


The next day, I met the guys at the clubhouse. I had my ghoul story in my backpack. Delmar had a can of Coke. And Amos had this big flashlight.

"What you looking for?" I asked him. "You think

there's buried treasure, or what?"

"I think there's something behind that door. That's what I think. And I'm kind of wondering what it is," Amos told me.

"The door's locked," Delmar said. He took a swig of his Coke, then took out a comic book.

"It was locked yesterday," Amos replied. "You never know about today. I mean, there's a lock on the door to our clubhouse, right? But second try, we got in here. So is that kind of weird, or what?"

I don't think we had ever thought about that. We just thought Amos was lucky. The outside door to the basement was a million-to-one chance, but he got lucky. It's like a slot machine, sometimes you get lucky. Besides, the clubhouse was so cool we didn't care. For a year, we fixed it up and came down every day. We had so much fun down here it seemed like a private club. We kept saying, not just rich kids get a private club.

But now Amos kept asking questions. "So how come we've never seen a mouse or a rat down here?"

"Nothing for them to eat," I said. "Besides, I hate rats."

"But we don't have no rats down here, and that's kind of weird. And now this door shows up, out of nowhere. I mean, one day there's a wall and the next day there's a door. That's kind of weird, too."

"So what's with the flashlight?" Delmar asked.

"It's just in case," Amos said. "We got just one light and two little windows here. Something goes wrong and we could get trapped down here in the dark. So I got the flashlight, just in case."

"And 'cause you want to look behind that door."

"Yeah," Amos said. He looked at the rest of us through his square glasses. "I'm not scared like you guys."

Well, that didn't bug me. I really was a bit scared. I'm scared of mice and rats, that's for sure, and I'm kind of scared of getting trapped in the dark. I never told the others, but I get nightmares sometimes. In the nightmare, I'm trapped in the clubhouse in the dark, and there's rats crawling over my feet.

But Delmar — nobody could ever tell Delmar he was scared. Not to his face, anyhow. So Delmar started cursing at Amos and calling him a wuss. Then Delmar got up and ran over to the weird door. He grabbed the handle, gave it a big twist and . . .

The door flew open.

"Holy ——!" Delmar said. And he doesn't curse much.

Amos and me, our jaws just dropped. We kept staring at that open door as if a monster was going to come out of there. For maybe a minute, all we could hear was our own breathing.

We were scared. All three of us were scared, but nobody would say a word. We just kept breathing and staring into the dark room beyond the door. I could feel cold air blowing out of there.

Finally, Delmar broke the silence.

"So are you wusses coming, or do I go in there by myself?"

"There could be rats," I said. Okay, so maybe I was a wuss, but there might be rats back there. We didn't know what might be back there.

"There's probably nothing, just like here," Amos said. He always had a good head on his shoulders. Chances were good that it was another big empty basement.

"I thought you brought the flashlight to go look," Delmar said.

"Yeah," Amos admitted.

"So stop being wusses and let's go look," Delmar said. "C'mon, you guys."

Amos got up and grabbed the big flashlight, then walked toward the door.

"You coming, Jamal?" Delmar asked. "Or are you a gutless dweeb?"

That didn't leave me much choice. I got up and ran to join the others. No way I was going to get left behind and have them calling me a gutless dweeb.

Amos got in front and turned on the flashlight. We still couldn't see much on the other side of the door. We could hardly see a thing until we took a few steps through the door.

It was quiet, damp and cold. The air smelled like wet earth. There seemed to be nothing in front of us but a big empty room.

"See, there's nothing," Delmas told us.

"Right," Amos replied, his voice a little shaky. "Nothing. Nothing at all."

But then the three of us froze. Maybe we couldn't see anything, but somehow we knew more than that. There *was* something there. Something we just couldn't see.

## CHAPTER THREE

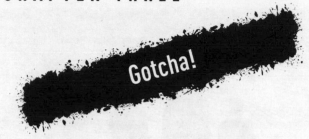

Gotcha!

**Amos kept shining** the light ahead of us. At first, there was nothing to see. It was as if the light was getting eaten up by the darkness.

At first.

But then our eyes got used to the dark. And then we all saw them, three white shapes way off in the room. They might have been smoke, because we could see right through them. But they still had a shape. Smoke rises up and it blows away — it's really nothing at all. But these three things were not

smoke. They did not blow in the cold, rushing air. They floated in front of us, with black holes where their eyes should have been.

We stared at them. Maybe, just maybe, they stared at us.

"What the . . . ?" Amos began. He didn't finish.

"Ghosts," I whispered.

"Ghouls," Delmar said.

The shapes began to move and the three of us fell

silent. The middle one rose up and floated over the shape on the right. Then the left shape started to come forward. Slowly, all three shapes began moving toward us.

The air was blowing at us and getting colder. It seemed to be coming from the shapes themselves. It smelled of dirt and death and the grave.

"Out of here," I whispered.

But then the door slammed shut behind us.

"Ohmygod!" Delmar cried.

We turned back, looking for the door. It was almost lost in the darkness. There was just a small glint of light from the handle. I took two steps back and grabbed for it.

The handle was like ice. It seemed frozen in my hand, or maybe my hand was frozen. I wasn't sure anymore. Nothing was making sense.

"Turn it," Delmar hissed.

"Can't," I croaked.

I looked back over my shoulder. The shapes had come halfway across the room. A few seconds more and they'd be on us.

I felt a hand touch my hand — and I screamed. But the hand wasn't from a ghost or a ghoul, it was Delmar's.

"Turn it!" he shouted.

I could feel him trying to twist my hand and the doorknob. But nothing moved. My hand and the doorknob were frozen.

Delmar swore. He took a step back toward the shapes, then took a running leap at the door.

SMASH!

I heard him smash against the door, his shoulder against the metal. The door shook and the handle twisted in my hand.

Then the door flew open.

"Move it," Delmar screamed. "Out of here. We gotta get out of here!"

Somehow I pulled my hand off the door handle. Somehow I found the strength to pull myself free and follow Delmar through the door.

In a second, we were both outside the room. We

were breathing like two guys who had run a 10K race.

Delmar grabbed at the door, getting ready to slam it closed. I was right beside him. It might take both of us to hold the door closed. It might take us all to keep the shapes — whatever they were — from getting out. But we didn't have all of us. There was only Delmar and me. Amos was still inside the room, still shining his light on the ghouls.

"Amos, get out of there!" Delmar yelled. "Move it!"

But Amos didn't move. The flashlight did not turn, or jiggle. It was as if Amos was frozen inside that room.

"Drop the light!" I screamed at him. "Run!"

But it was too late. The door began to move — all on its own. The door between Amos and us, between us and the things, slammed shut.

"Amos!" Delmar screamed.

"Pull!" I told Delmar.

The two of us grabbed the door handle and

twisted, but the handle spun in our hands. We pulled with all our strength, but the door was locked shut. It might as well have been welded into its frame.

"We gotta get help," I shouted. "They got Amos! We gotta get help!"

Delmar and I ran out of our clubhouse. We ran as fast as we'd ever run in our lives. We had to find somebody to help us. We had to do something — the ghouls had Amos!

# CHAPTER FOUR

Crying Wolf?

We ran like crazy, like nutbars. We ran down Canal and Gerrard until we got to the rec center. Delmar was ahead of me. He threw the door open and we both ran up to the desk.

A kid named Joey looked at us like *we* were ghouls.

"Help!" Delmar panted. "We gotta get help."

"Call somebody!" I shouted. "Call 911!"

Joey picked up the phone, then he asked us the big question. "What happened, man?"

"The ghouls," Delmar told him. "The ghouls got Amos!"

Joey shot us a look as he called 911. That should have been our first clue. That look should have told us what we'd be in for.

By the time the cops got there, we'd already told Joey and his boss. They kept giving us this look, like, *what are you guys trying to pull?* And these were guys who knew us. I mean, I'm not a joker. I don't pull pranks. I don't B.S. people just for a laugh. We had a real problem, and these guys had to know it.

But not the cops.

"Okay, what's the problem here?" said the first cop. There were two of them: a young cop who looked Spanish and an old fat cop with white hair. They both gave us a look.

"It's our friend, Amos," I began. "The ghouls got him."

"The ghouls?" said the fat cop. And then we got that look, again.

"Yeah, we were over at our clubhouse," Delmar told them. "And there was this new door. Like, we'd never seen it before. So we opened it and went inside and, well, there they were."

"The ghouls," said the young cop.

"Yeah, the ghouls," I told him. I could see these guys wouldn't believe us. The looks on their faces said it all. They didn't even pull out a notebook. It was like this was all some big joke.

Delmar didn't give up. "Anyhow, we went inside and we saw the ghouls. So we ran, but, like, Amos held back. And he had the flashlight. And then the ghouls got him."

"They got him," repeated the young cop.

"Yeah, they got him," I said.

"So did the ghouls eat him, or what?" asked the fat cop. And then the young cop kind of laughed. So did Joey.

"We don't know," I told both of them. "The door slammed shut, and there was no way we could get back in. So we ran here and then called 911."

"To report the ghouls?" asked the young cop.

"No, man, to get Amos out. We need help!"

This was worse than awful. Our friend was locked in a basement. Our friend was trapped with the ghouls. And these guys just laughed at us, like it was all a joke. They were moving in slow motion. I mean, these cops hustle faster to get to Tim Hortons.

We spent a long time in the car, filling out some paperwork. Delmar and me had to beg the guys to even get out of the car. Then we had to beg them to come with us to the warehouse. It was like pulling teeth to get them to do anything!

We took them down the steps then pressed the buttons to get in. The old cop didn't like this. He wanted to know how we knew the numbers. Then the young cop asked who let us use the place. For a while, it was like we were doing a B&E and they were going to take us down for it.

And when we got to our clubhouse, it all got worse.

"Okay," said the young cop, "your friend went

where?"

"There," Delmar said, pointing. "Through the door."

Delmar pointed and we all looked . . . but there was no door. There was nothing on that wall but concrete blocks. There was no door, no nothing.

"What door?" asked the old cop.

"The door that was there, on that wall," I said. I could feel my heart sinking into my shoes. I mean, we sounded nuts. If I'd been listening to me, I'd say that I was crazy. Maybe I was crazy. I mean, how can you tell? All we could tell, for sure, is that the far wall didn't have a door.

"So your friend went into that wall?" said the young cop.

"Yeah," I sighed. "We all went through the door . . . the one that isn't there anymore."

The young cop laughed. He tried to hold it back. I mean, cops aren't allowed to laugh or get mad or make jokes. Cops should take you seriously. But I guess it was all too much. So the young cop laughed a little, and then the fat cop laughed.

"It happened," Delmar said.

"It did," I added. "Really, it did."

"This isn't some Halloween prank, is it?" asked the young cop. "I mean, it's not Halloween, guys. A joke is a joke, but you're really wasting police time on this."

The two cops gave us a new look. It wasn't like they were mad at us. They just thought we were nuts. They thought we should be in some loony bin.

"Listen," I said. I was starting to lose it. "We've got a missing person. Door or no door, our friend Amos is missing. He went through that wall, with us, and he never came out."

The young cop looked at me hard, then he had an idea. "Okay, so let's call Amos's house and see what's up. How about that?"

So Delmar gave him the phone number. He pulled out a cell phone and hit the numbers. In the silent basement, we heard the phone ring at Amos's place.

"Hello," said the cop. "We're trying to reach the parent of Amos Brown. Yes, ma'am. Thank you." And then the cop went into this long thing about who he was, and all that. "We have a report that your son is a missing person. Would you have . . . "

There was a lot of talk coming through the phone. It sounded like Amos' mom had something to say.

"So you say he's taking a nap, Mrs. Brown?" the cop said. "Would you mind just going to check?"

We waited. I think both Delmar and me knew what the answer would be. We both knew that Amos would be in his bedroom, sleeping like a log. We both knew we'd end up looking crazy.

"Hello, Amos," the cop went on. "A couple of your buddies thought you were in trouble. You know two guys named Jamal and Delmar?"

There was another voice. It must have been Amos.

"They thought you were in some trouble," said the cop, "so we're just checking. Sorry to wake you up."

He pushed the end button and put his phone away. Then there was this awful silence. The cops looked at us, and we looked down . . . or at the wall. It was the old cop who broke the silence.

"You know, you two could be in real trouble," he began. And then we got the whole speech. The cops could have thrown the book at us. We wasted their time. We upset our friend's family. We got the staff at the rec center all upset. And we could be charged for breaking into the basement.

"But it's our clubhouse," Delmar whined.

"I'm just saying," said the old cop. "You could be charged. That doesn't mean we're going to charge you. But I'm going to write this up, and I don't want it to happen again. You ever heard the story of the boy who cried wolf?"

We shook our heads.

"You ask your teachers, they'll tell you. Anyhow, we're going to let this one go. But don't be coming down here again. That's a B&E if we find you down here, unless you get the owner to say it's okay. So take our advice, go hang out at the rec center. You won't get in trouble with us that way."

Then the young cop added. "And you won't have to worry about the ghouls coming to get you."

# CHAPTER FIVE

The First Rat

So maybe we didn't get into big trouble. The cops let us off with a warning. But the guys at the rec center thought we were nuts. And Amos's mom thought we were nuts.

But the big problem was us. Even Delmar and me couldn't figure it all out. There was a door, and we went through it, and then there wasn't one. Amos was with us, and then he wasn't, and then he was back at his house. None of this added up. It was nuts.

Then I got home and all my mom could say was, "Jamal, where you been?"

I didn't tell her. But I did call Amos and he swore — he swore on a stack of Bibles — that he'd been home. "I was sick," he told me. "I got sick to my stomach at school and had to leave early. Then I got home and really threw up. I fell on my bed and had these weird dreams. But there's no way I was down at the clubhouse."

"Serious?" I asked

"Serious," he said.

"So what kind of dreams?"

"Weird ones. The ghouls were in them. I woke up once when they were gonna eat my face."

"Nice," I told him.

"Yeah, but here's the funny thing. They didn't want me," Amos said. "Not in the dream, anyhow. I was the wrong guy, or something like that. They were looking for somebody else."

It was another one of those *Twilight Zone* things. You know, the music plays in your head and you get this feeling in your spine. The ghouls were looking for somebody else. Was it me? Was it Delmar?

The next day, we were going to meet at the clubhouse but Amos was still sick. His mom said he had some kind of flu. So Delmar and me, we went to the rec center to hang out. It's not that we were scared. No way. It's just that the cops told us we'd be in trouble if we went to the clubhouse. And besides, the place was feeling real creepy.

But the rec center wasn't so hot, either. Joey had told all the guys about what happened. The word was out: Delmar and I were loony tunes. We got in the gym and you could tell by the looks. And then the words:

"Hey, man, you seen any spooks lately?"

"What's the matter, Jamal? Can't handle a little ghoul or two?"

Or just guys going "Boo!" to see if we'd jump.

So the next day we were back at the clubhouse after school. The lock numbers were the same, so I guess the police hadn't said anything to the owners.

Anyhow, we got in just like always.

Amos was still looking a little sick. I mean, you could make a joke, like, "Amos, you look like you've seen a ghost!" But the three of us, we weren't joking. We all saw the ghouls, all three of us. Maybe nobody would believe us, but we saw them. And we saw the door, all three of us. We weren't loony tunes, just guys who saw what we saw.

"So Amos," Delmar began, "what was it like? What did the ghouls do to you?"

Amos shook his head. "I told you, it was just a dream. You guys have both got weird since then."

That's when Delmar and me got mad. "Amos, you were here, man," I told him. "You were here with us, and you saw the door. And you saw the ghouls."

"Yeah, I remember the door," Amos said. "It was right, like, there." He pointed at the concrete block wall. "We all saw the door, and it was locked. You tried the door, and it was locked."

"Right," I said. "So two days ago you came back

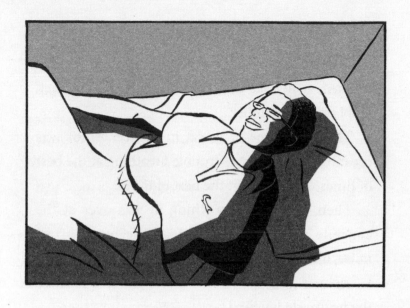

with us. You had this big flashlight, remember?"

There was a blank look on Amos's face.

"And we tried the door," Delmar went on, "and it flew open. Remember that? We went inside, to the other room, and that's when we saw the ghouls."

"Yeah, in my dream," Amos said.

"Not in your ——— dream!" Delmar screamed. He really cursed, too. "Here! It happened right *here!*"

Delmar was really mad. Amos looked like he was

going to cry. And I just felt kind of stupid.

"I don't remember, guys," Amos said. His voice cracked — he was that close to crying. "I got sick and I don't remember."

Then the three of us sat in silence. Amos was breathing hard. He has trouble breathing at the best of times. This was not the best of times.

Then we heard something. It was over at the concrete wall. There was this little brush-brush noise, like something moving on the floor.

Delmar grabbed Amos's flashlight and pointed the beam. He laughed.

"Your favorite thing, Jamal," he said. "Rats."

I shivered. I don't know what it is about rats, but they really get to me. And we'd been lucky with the clubhouse. We'd never seen a rat down here before.

Delmar picked up a piece of concrete and threw it at the rat. The thing ran off into the corner.

"Give me something else to throw," Delmar said.

Amos gave him a tennis ball.

"Gonna have rat guts on this ball when I get

him," Delmar said.

"You can't kill a rat with a tennis ball," Amos said.

"Just watch me," Delmar snapped back. "You hold the light. I'm gonna get a little closer."

I just sat on this beat-up chair we had, holding my legs up. I mean, who knew where the rat was going to run? The last thing I wanted was him running over my feet, or crawling up my leg.

Delmar got up and walked a couple of steps

toward the corner. It was dark back there, but Amos kept pointing the light.

"Come on, little guy," Delmar said, talking to the rat. "Just come out and we'll play some tennis. Just let me see your cute little rat face. Come on, now . . ."

Again, there was the brush-brush sound of the rat running. It was hard to see him. I mean, a rat is grey and the concrete wall is grey and the light wasn't all that good. But you could hear the rat running.

Delmar was watching hard. He kept looking into the darkness.

Then we all saw the thing. This was one big rat, almost the size of my foot. No way that Delmar was going to take him out with a tennis ball.

But Delmar never got the chance. The rat stopped, turned, and seemed to look at us. Then he sniffed a couple times, turned again, and was gone.

He had squeezed under the door. Not the door to outside, but the green metal door that led to the ghouls.

The door was back! It was the same door, but in a new place. Now it was in the corner of the room, and we all knew what was behind it.

"Holy ———!" Delmar screamed. His voice was way up high, like he was scared out of his mind. "We gotta get out of here!"

# CHAPTER SIX

Ghouls Return

I don't think Amos ever moved so fast in his life. I mean, the guy is not a track star. He's always at the back of the pack when we run in gym. The only guy slower than him is Fat Jackson, and Fat Jackson is really, really fat.

But Amos was at the exit door like lightning. He was faster than Delmar and he was way faster than me.

"Go, go, go!" Delmar said.

"I'm going!" Amos told him. He kept turning the

door handle, but nothing happened.

"Here, let me," Delmar told him. Then he pushed Amos to one side and began twisting the handle. Nothing. Delmar swore. Then he began pulling on the handle with all his might. Delmar is a pretty big guy. When he put his foot on the door frame and yanked, he really pulled.

He pulled so hard, the handle came off in his hand. He flew backward until he was sprawled on the floor. The handle was still in his hand. A little blood was coming from a cut on his lip.

"I don't like this," Amos said, his voice all high and scared.

"Neither do I," I told him.

And then it all got worse.

The door in the corner of the room slammed open. We couldn't see a thing in the corner. The room beyond the door was pitch black. But the door was open and something funny was happening.

It was as if the darkness beyond the door was coming out at us. I don't know any better way to

explain it. The blackness beyond the door spread into the corner, then it flowed into the room. It was like black smoke, but it wasn't smoke. It was just darkness, just blackness.

"Holy ———!" Delmar cried out again. He got up on his feet and joined us by the exit door. "What are we gonna do?"

"You know how to pray?" I asked him.

"No," he said.

"Then learn quick, man, 'cause I'm starting to pray right now."

I didn't fall to my knees, but I started talking to God. I mean, I had a hunch what was back there. I had a hunch what was coming next. And I didn't like either one of those.

The lamp we had in our clubhouse went off. The flashlight on the floor went off.

Amos started to cry. He was sobbing and blubbering like a little kid. "No, not me," he begged. "Not again. Don't take me there again. Please. I don't want to go."

"What are you talking about?" I asked him.

But Amos was beyond talking. He was crying and shaking like some guy in a movie. I mean, there are words like "terror" that you read in books, but you don't see it much in real life. But I looked at Amos and that word became real. Amos's face was a face of terror. I don't think a human being could be more scared and still be alive.

And then it got darker.

The basement had these little windows up at shoulder height. They weren't much as windows go. There were four of them, each about the size of a mid-size TV screen. In the afternoon, they let in just enough light so we could come in and turn on the lamp. Up until a minute ago, they gave us enough light to see.

But now the windows were getting darker. It was like a big cloud had covered the sun. The windows got darker . . . and darker . . . and darker. In maybe thirty seconds, the windows were just dull black rectangles.

Our clubhouse was pitch black. Amos was crying and shaking. Delmar was swearing and pounding on the door to outside. I just stood there, waiting for what would come next.

Then they appeared. Slowly. Silently.

We all saw them at the same time. The ghouls were in the corner, floating. They hadn't come out of the door. They just seemed to appear, all at the same time.

Amos screamed.

I thought I was going to pee my pants.

But Delmar went nuts. He rushed over to the big couch and grabbed our big lamp. Then he picked up the lamp, ripped off the shade and smashed the lamp on the floor. The light bulb smashed, leaving jagged edges of glass at the end of the lamp.

Delmar held the lamp like a sword or a lance, in both hands. He aimed the jagged end at the ghouls.

"I'm not going without a fight," he told them. His voice was shaking and he was breathing hard, but you could hear the strength in his voice. "If you want me, you got a fight on your hands. You hear me? Can you talk, or what?"

The ghouls gave no answer at first. All I could hear was Amos sobbing, Delmar breathing, and the awful beating of my own heart.

Then one ghoul moved forward. There was a change in its shape. There seemed to be a hole in the whiteness, and then the hole became a mouth . . . and then the hole had teeth. The ghoul's mouth had enormous, pointy teeth.

That's when I peed my pants.

Delmar swore.

Amos began saying, "No, no, no. Not me, not me. Not again. Please, please, not me." It was like a chant, repeated over and over again.

The ghouls began to float toward us. I backed away, over to the right. Amos stayed where he was, his body rocking, his words repeating. "No, no, no. Please, please not me."

Delmar held the broken lamp out in front of him. "C'mon, you ———. I'm ready for you. C'mon."

From over our heads, there came a laugh. It was a deep laugh that came like an echo from a long way away. But it was loud, so loud my ears hurt. Maybe it was coming from the ghoul with the mouth. Maybe it was coming from all three of them. Maybe it was coming from the walls or the ceiling.

Laughter. Awful, insane laughter.

I backed to the far wall, just under one dark

window. I picked up a chunk of concrete block from the floor. Maybe Delmar had the right idea. Maybe the best thing was to fight back. Maybe before they got us, we could hurt them. Maybe we could take them out.

The ghouls got to Delmar first. The middle one, the one with the mouth, seemed to focus on him. Its white shape seemed to reform. Now there was a mouth and eyes and a head and one arm. The arm was reaching out toward Delmar.

"C'mon, you ———. C'mon!"

Delmar jabbed at the ghoul with the lamp. The ghoul reached out and seemed to surround the lamp. For a second, nothing happened. It all seemed frozen, like a freeze frame in the movies.

Then the laughter was gone and there was a new sound — a buzz — like something electric.

Delmar was frozen. And then he screamed.

"NOOOOO!"

Delmar started to shake. It was like an electric current was running through his body. He was shaking and twisting and shrieking "No" at the top of his lungs.

Then the buzz stopped and Delmar fell to the floor. He wasn't moving.

Again, we heard laughter. The three ghouls began moving forward again. They floated right over Delmar's body. Then they split up — one headed toward Amos, two coming at me.

"No, no, no. Please, not me," Amos begged.

The ghoul kept coming at him.

I looked at the two ghouls coming toward me. Bad odds. Even if they were human, I didn't like the odds.

I remembered my dad, before he went off to prison. He used to say, "There's a time to fight and a time to run. A smart guy knows the difference." My dad wasn't so smart. Maybe that's why he was in prison. But I had to get smart, fast, so I made my choice.

I still had the half-block of concrete in my hand. But I knew it was useless against these things. So I ran to the farthest window, to get the most time. Then I held the brick at the back and smashed at the center of the window. It cracked and a piece of glass shot outside. Suddenly there was more light in the room.

I could see Amos down on his knees, still chanting. His ghoul had surrounded him. Amos was disappearing into a white cloud.

But I had no time to watch. There was no more time to worry about Amos or Delmar, I had to save myself. I took the concrete block and kept smashing at the glass, knocking out piece after piece. Finally I had a pretty big hole in the glass, big enough to fit through.

The ghouls were close, not even a few feet away. But they weren't moving fast. I tried to smash the last bits of glass at the edge, the jagged ones, but then I ran out of time.

I stepped up on a ledge and stuck my head through the hole. Then I grabbed the window frame — jagged edges too — and pulled myself up.

I was doing good, real good. Pain was shooting up from my hands where they'd been cut by the glass. Another piece of glass was ripping through my shirt and into my chest. But my head and my shoulders were out in real air. I was breathing real air. There was no more awful laughter coming from all around me. I just had to get the rest of me through.

So I pulled until I was almost clear. My belt got stuck on the window frame, but then I pushed myself through. I was almost out. I pulled my left leg through. My stupid running shoe got stuck. So I wiggled the shoe and got it free.

I was almost clear, almost free. I began pulling my right leg through the window, but suddenly it felt very, very cold. It was like going to the dentist when he puts freezing in your gums. My leg felt cold and weak. I could almost feel the muscles in that leg losing strength.

*C'mon, Jamal,* I told myself. *Pull that sucker. Pull.*

My leg had no strength left, but my arms were

good. I grabbed at some weeds in front of me and pulled my whole body — legs and all — forward. I could feel the ghouls pulling my right leg. They were trying to pull me back in.

*You can do this, Jamal. You're almost there.*

I pulled harder. There were tears running down my cheeks and blood all over my hands. But I pulled on those weeds like my life depended on it.

Maybe my life did depend on it.

At last my right leg came free. The ghoul that was holding it let go, and I fell outside onto the ground.

I was hurt — bad — but I was free!

# CHAPTER SEVEN

Believe Me!

I crawled across the ground. My right leg felt like it was frozen, kind of tingling. It was as if I didn't have any control over it. It kind of dragged behind me as I moved. I got up on my feet and tried to walk, but my right leg wouldn't take my weight. So I put my weight on my left leg and kind of moved forward. There's a word for that — hobbled, that's the word. I remembered that dumb word from Mr. Donkey's class. Hobbled.

And then I thought about my friends. Amos and

Delmar were still back there, still trapped with the ghouls. I could imagine . . . I can't tell you what I could imagine.

At the edge of the street, I fell down and sat on a curb. I was still scared, still looking back over my shoulder. But there were other people around now. Some of the warehouse guys were driving home. A couple of them looked at me from their cars.

What they saw was a frightened kid, all covered with dirt and blood. I was bleeding from my mouth, my hands and my chest. I was filthy from the dirt, the window and crawling along the ground.

Did anybody stop? No way. I was just some dirty black kid sitting on the curb. The guys in the cars, they'd look at me, then look away. Maybe they were afraid I was going to beg for money. Maybe they thought I was going to steal their cars. But nobody stopped.

For a little while, I thought about running in .front of a car and shouting for help. I thought about begging one of those guys to call the cops. But then

I thought about what the cops would say. *Why were you back down in the basement? Didn't we tell you to stay out of there? Didn't you pull this stunt before? This time we're going to charge you, kid.*

But I couldn't just do nothing. My friends were trapped back there. They were fighting for their lives . . . if they were still alive at all. I had to find somebody who would help me.

So I pulled myself up from the curb. My right leg was a little better, but I still walked with a limp. So I limped down the street, past the rec center, until I saw our school.

It was almost six o'clock, so the school was pretty empty. There were only a handful of cars in the lot. The kids and teachers had mostly gone home. Night school wouldn't begin for another hour or so. But the front door opened as I was still limping my way up the steps.

It was Lee, that white chick who's so hot about dancing. She had on a kind of dancer outfit, so she must have been coming from a practice. I had known Lee for a long time, back when she was still Bonnie Lee — a skinny kid with pigtails. That was years ago, but Lee would remember me. She'd help me. She'd *have* to help me.

Lee saw me the same time I saw her. "Jamal, what happened to you? You look like you've been in a fight."

"Yeah, kind of," I said quietly. *Should I tell her?* I wondered. *Would she believe me?* "Listen, I've got a real problem. I guess you can see that, eh?"

"Yeah, I can see," Lee replied. "It looks like you just got beat up. I mean, what kind of trouble are you in?"

I could hear a little fear in her voice. The white kids are like that. They look at us black guys and think we're all gangbangers. They think we've got guns under our pillows and drugs in our backpacks. It's all the stuff they see on TV, and 'cause they don't really know us. They've got their own world — the country club up in the park. And we've got our world — the streets. So I knew why Lee would be scared, even if she wasn't one of those rich white kids. She just didn't know us that well.

"Okay, I'll try to keep this short because I got some friends that need help," I began. "It all started last week . . ."

So I told her about the clubhouse, and the strange door, and Amos disappearing. Then I told her about the cops, and us going back, and the door in the corner. I kind of left out the ghouls, because that's the crazy part. When I told Joey and the rec center guys and the cops about the ghouls, that's when they all stopped listening.

"So your friends are stuck down there?" Lee asked. "I mean, you got out through a window. So how come Amos and Delmar didn't get out?"

I looked down at the steps. "Because of . . . stuff?"

"What stuff?" Lee went on. "You tell me this great big story, but you're leaving something out. If you want help, Jamal, I've got to know the whole thing."

"Yeah, well, I know that. But nobody believes this part . . . and I don't want you to think I'm crazy. I'm not making this up. It happened."

"What happened?" she demanded.

"There are ghouls down there. Ghouls or ghosts or something . . . something not human."

That kind of stopped her cold. She gave me this look, searching my face. Maybe she thought I was joking. Maybe she was checking to see if this was all a big joke. Lee even looked around, maybe to see if there was a hidden camera. I mean, this is the kind of thing they do for the *Just For Laughs* videos.

Except this wasn't a joke. It wasn't a funny video. It was real.

"Okay," she sighed. "So you think the ghouls, or ghosts, or whatever, have got your friends. That's what you think, right?"

"Yeah," I told her. "It's what I *know*." I put a lot of weight into that word *know*.

"So let's say I believe you," she went on. I was pretty sure she didn't believe me, but at least she didn't start laughing. "Let's say that the ghouls have your friends. Let me just check out that part." Lee pulled out her cell phone. "Okay, give me Amos's phone number."

So she called Amos's house. I could only hear one side of what they said. "Mrs. Brown . . . Oh, just a friend from school. Is Amos there? . . . Do you know where he might be? . . . No, I'm with Jamal . . . Okay, just tell him Lee called."

I could figure out the other side. Then I gave her the number for Delmar. His little brother answered the phone. Same story. Delmar wasn't there.

Lee closed her phone. "You could still be setting me up, Jamal. No way I'm going to follow you down into some warehouse. I mean, how stupid do you think I am?"

*She's right*, I thought to myself. Lee knew me from school, but she didn't *know* me, if you get my meaning. She was street smart, too. You had to be street smart in the hood.

"So don't follow me," I told her. "You got a cell

phone. Just keep that ready. I'll go back down into the basement on my own."

"And then what?" Lee asked.

"I'll try to save my friends," I told her.

"Like how?"

"I don't know how," I said. "I'll figure that out when I find the guys."

She shook her head. "So what do I do?"

"Wait ten minutes. If I come out . . . I mean, if *we* come out, then it's cool. No problem. We'll owe you big time. You need help with that big dance show, we'll be there. Anything you want, you got it."

"And if you don't come out?"

"Call the cops," I told her. "You're white, you're a girl and you know how to talk good. Just say help and they'll be there in two seconds flat. You don't have to tell them about the ghouls, or anything. Just say it was a gang meeting or something. I mean, you're smarter than me. You'll figure out something."

"This is crazy," she said.

"I know," I told her. "But it's the truth. I got nobody else to help me, just you. Do I have to get on my knees and beg?"

She looked at me. I think she was trying to see if this was all a big con. I think she was worried about me and my friends. Maybe, just maybe, she was worried about the ghouls. I mean, there was a lot to think about.

"Okay, I'll help you out," she said. "But I've got a 911 button on this phone, Jamal. If you or your guys try something funny, I'll have the cops on you. They'll nail you faster than I can do a *jete*. You get what I'm saying?"

I got up and smiled. "Don't know what a *jete* is, but I get the idea. Let's go."

I wasn't really sure what I could do back in the basement, but at least I had some backup. At least I could try to save my friends.

## CHAPTER EIGHT

Back Through the Door

It took maybe ten minutes to get back to Canal Street. By now, it was starting to get dark out. Lee kept looking around at the old warehouses, like somebody might jump out at her.

I wasn't afraid of that. I was afraid of what was under one warehouse. I was afraid of what might be in our old clubhouse. And I was afraid of what the ghouls might be doing to my friends . . . and to me.

I wasn't limping so bad now. My leg still dragged, but I could move it. Lee walked fast, and I could keep up.

We didn't talk anymore. Lee had this stern look on her face. I guess part of her felt stupid for coming with me. And part of her was worried about the gangs in this part of the hood. And part of her maybe believed what I said. Maybe she worried that the ghouls would come after her, too.

I saw myself in a window as we walked past. I was a mess. I looked like a car had run over me. My clothes were filthy. There was dried blood on my shirt and my face. And there was a big stain on my pants. I didn't look good, and I didn't smell good either. I was lucky that Lee wasn't too close to me.

I tried to make some plan for going back down. My first problem was light. How could I see down there with no light? Then I remembered Amos' flashlight. That was down there, somewhere. And there'd be a little light from the door to outside and the windows. That should be enough light to see. If

the guys were still there, then I could drag them outside.

If . . . if . . .

What if the guys weren't there? What if the ghouls had dragged them beyond the door?

No way I was going in there by myself. I mean, that would be crazy. I'd get myself killed . . . or worse. Maybe I'd just come out and get Lee to phone for help. Maybe the cops would believe her.

But Lee didn't really believe me. I didn't have any proof. I couldn't prove that my friends were with me. I had no proof that the ghouls had come at us. I had nothing, nothing at all. The cops would just throw me into the loony bin. My friends would be stuck, or dead, or worse.

"Okay, Jamal," Lee said, "we're here."

"Yeah, this is it," I told her. "The basement stairs are over here."

I led her around to the side of the building. There were four stairs down to the basement door.

"This is as far as I go, Jamal," Lee told me. She was standing way back from the basement stairs, looking all around. She already had the cell phone open and ready.

I could tell she was scared. I figure she was more scared of me and my friends than of the ghouls. She had a lot of guts to come with me this far.

"Yeah, okay," I told her. "I understand. The rest is up to me."

"So now what?"

"I'm going inside," I told her. I was pushing the buttons on the lock. "I'm going to prop the door open. If this thing slams shut, you call the cops."

"Right," she said.

"Just call the cops. Whatever you do, don't come after me. Got that?"

"Got it," she said.

I twisted the door handle with my hand. It pulled open, no problem. Inside, our old clubhouse was black. It took a minute for my eyes to get used to the dark.

"Here," Lee said, reaching down to me. "Take this."

She gave me a little flashlight, one of those MAG lights. It was really bright.

"Thanks," I said.

"And I've got an idea," she told me. "I've got a clock on my cell. I'm going to shout out your name each minute. If you're okay, you shout back 'okay.' If you don't shout back, I'll call the police. Got that."

"Okay," I said.

"And if things get bad, you shout out 'help.' Don't try to be a hero, Jamal."

"Right."

"One more thing," she said. "No matter what happens, I'm not going down into that basement. I'll call the cops. I'll try to get help. But no way I'm going in after you. Got that?"

"Right."

"And one more thing," Lee went on. "If this is all a sick joke, you're in big trouble, Jamal. I've got friends . . ."

"Yeah," I said. "I get the message."

"Good."

She gave me a look, like I was stalling or soemthing. And maybe I was. I took a deep breath.

"Okay, I'm going in."

I flipped on the MAG light and walked through the basement door.

# CHAPTER NINE

An Invitation

"Jamal, you okay?"

I walked into our clubhouse. No, it was the place that used to be our clubhouse. Now it was just a dirty old basement. I could see the floor lamp that Delmar had smashed. I could see Amos' flashlight on the floor. But that was it. The old carpet was gone. Our couch and chairs were gone. It was like we'd never had a clubhouse here. It was like the last year had never happened.

"Jamal, you okay?" I heard again.

"Yeah, I'm okay," I shouted back.

Was I really okay? No, I was scared to death. There was sweat running off my face and down my back. But the basement was cold, dead cold. There was plenty of light coming from the door, the windows and the flashlight. But it was still hard to see much.

I ran my flashlight over the walls, looking for the door. I knew the door could move. I knew the door could be anywhere. But I saw nothing. Nothing but a grey shape crawling along the floor.

*A rat*, I said to myself. And then I shivered some more.

"Jamal, you okay?"

"Fine," I shouted. "Just peachy!" A little joke, of course. I figured if I could laugh or smile that might help.

I walked farther into the basement. I was right in the center of it, right where our carpet should have been. I aimed the MAG light at the far wall. Nothing. I twisted the flashlight to make a small beam. I'd just go over the walls, carefully. The door had to be there. An hour ago, the door was right there. Now my friends were behind it.

Nothing on that wall. I turned to the next. It seemed to me that I could hear breathing. But when I stopped to listen, the sound was gone.

I could see the window I had smashed. The glass was still jagged, still pretty mean. But there was no door on that wall. Nothing at all.

So I turned to the next wall. That's where the door had been that first day. I aimed right at the spot where the door had been. Nothing.

And then I felt something touch my leg. It was a gentle touch, kind of fuzzy. I aimed the flashlight beam down at my feet.

"YAAAAH!" I screamed.

"Jamal, what happened?" Lee yelled.

"Nothing," I shouted back. "Just a rat. I hate rats," I told her.

We never used to have rats down here. That was pretty strange, now that I think about it. But I'd never seen a rat until last week. Now there was a rat at one wall. And another rat had run right by my feet — a big one. I mean, if I could feel the rat touch my leg it must be as big as a small dog.

I shivered again.

I turned my flashlight to the last wall. I ran it over the concrete blocks, left to right, top to bottom. Nothing. No door. Nothing at all.

I was ready to give up and leave when I heard something. It was a kind of brush-brush sound. *Another rat,* I said to myself. I pointed the flashlight at the sound. There, in the corner, I saw a little grey shape. Then two shapes, crawling near the wall. More rats. Beyond them a I saw a little hole where the wall met the floor. There was a third rat coming out of the hole.

I shivered. I wanted to throw up.

"Jamal, you okay?" Lee yelled.

"I'm coming out," I told her. "Nothing here but rats."

I turned toward the door and started to walk. I

kept the flashlight aimed at the floor. I didn't want to step on a rat on my way out.

But then a big wind came out of nowhere. The door — the door I had propped open with a concrete block — slammed shut.

I turned fast, looking all around me. No door. No ghouls. Just rats coming out of the hole in the wall.

"Lee, phone the cops!" I shouted. "Get me out of here!" My voice was way up high. It was more like a squeak than my real voice.

I heard nothing back. I heard nothing at all except the brush-brush of the rats. There seemed to be ten or twenty of them. They were pouring out of the hole, then running along the walls.

I looked over the window that I'd broken. I had climbed out once — I could climb out again. But under the window there were a dozen rats. They were on the floor, even on the wall. I'd have to fight my way through the rats to reach the window.

Did I have a choice? I looked around for some weapon to hit the rats. The only thing I could find was the broken lamp on the floor. It wasn't much, but it was better than using my bare hands.

I picked up the lamp. I remembered how Delmar had used it. I remembered the way he dared the ghouls to come at him. Where was Delmar now? What had they done with him?

Okay, it was time. I aimed the light back at the window. Now there were two dozen rats. The wall and the floor seemed to be covered with rats — small ones, big ones, rats the size of my shoes and rats the size of small dogs.

I wanted to throw up.

"Lee, can you hear me?" I screamed.

No answer.

*You gotta do this, Jamal,* I told myself. *You can't just wait here until the rats get you. You can't just stay here until the ghouls come back.*

"But we're already back," came a voice.

"What?" I screamed. Somebody was reading my thoughts. Somebody could look right inside my head.

"Who's that?" I aimed the flashlight all around the room. There were rats, everywhere, but that's all.

"Who are you?" I yelled. "What do you want?"

"We want you, Jamal," came the voice.

"Why?" I screamed. "What for? Look, I don't know nothing. I just want my friends. I just want to get out of here."

"We *are* your friends, Jamal," said the voice.

Then I saw something . . . in the corner. It was the door, the door in the wall. But the door was already open. There were shapes coming out of the door. I could see them coming out, one after the other. They were floating, like smoke, but more solid than that.

And there were five of them.

"Lee!" I screamed. "Get help!"

"She can't hear you, Jamal," said one of the ghouls. "She's gone. We scared her away. No one can hear you but us."

Then another ghoul spoke. "Us and the rats."

They laughed. I couldn't believe it. The ghouls

actually laughed.

I turned away from them, looking back at the broken window. Now there were hundreds of rats. They swarmed over the floor and over the wall. I shivered in disgust.

"You don't like rats, do you?" said one ghoul.

Again, the five of them laughed.

They were all coming at me. I could see them, floating in the air. They had bodies but no bodies, faces but no faces. The ghouls floated up over me, their teeth shining white in the dark.

Then I heard a voice from somewhere over my head. "We want you, too, Jamal. Your friends are with us. Now we want you."

I screamed. I ran back to the exit door, trying to get out, but it didn't work. There was no handle, and there was nothing to hold onto. The door didn't budge.

And then I got freezing cold, just like the basement all around me.

The ghouls came closer. I could see their breath, white in the air. I could see their teeth, their sharp pointy teeth, getting closer to me. I pulled back. I tried to put one arm up to hold them back, but it was hopeless. I was trapped against the door. The ghouls kept coming at me. It was dark, pitch dark, and all I could see was their teeth.

"No!" I screamed.

"Come join us," said the one ghoul. "Don't be afraid, Jamal. It's good. It's all good. Just ask Delmar. Just ask Amos. Your friends will tell you."

Then I heard a scream. It was the most terrible scream I had ever heard in my life. It was full of terror, and defeat, and suffering. It was the scream of someone who had fought hard, but was now dying in some terrible, cruel way. In that scream I could hear fear, despair and death . . . all at once.

And then I felt the ghoul's icy hand touch my shoulder.

## CHAPTER TEN

C'mon, Jamal

"Jamal," I heard. "Jamal."

Crazy thoughts were spinning around in my head. There was darkness and light. The shapes of the ghouls, their pointy teeth. And under all that was the cold. The ghoul's touch had sent cold into my body. The cold stung me, like the freezing you get at the dentist. I couldn't fight. I couldn't move. I couldn't breathe.

"Jamal, get up!"

"Huh . . . what?" I was dazed. I was frozen, cold,

almost dead. I couldn't breathe.

"Wake up, boy," I heard. It was my mother's voice. "You got the sheet all twisted around your head. Come on and wake up."

I fought against the white sheet around me. At last, my head pulled free. I opened my eyes and saw my bedroom. At the door was my mother.

"Don't know what you been dreaming about, Jamal. You been shouting all night. You were loud enough to wake the dead."

"What was I shouting about?"

My mom stood there and shook her head. "Something about a girl named Lee and something real scary. Must have really wiped you out. You didn't even wake up when the alarm went off."

"The alarm . . ." None of this was making sense. "How'd I get here?"

My mother just gave me a look, one of *those* looks. "How you think you got here, boy? Now get up out of bed and get moving. Your buddy Amos is waitin.'"

She closed the door, laughing at something.

I sat up in bed and pulled the sheet off me. Then I looked around. Same bedroom as always. Nothing had changed. No rats. No ghouls. Just my junky clothes on the floor and my pile of DVDs on the desk and my books in one corner. I could hear my little brother in the bathroom. He was talking to himself, the way he does.

"C'mon, Jamal," I heard from the living room. It was Amos's voice. "We gotta move, man."

So I got out of bed and went down the hall to the bathroom. I yelled at my brother Shaq to get out, and then splashed water on my face. Put a little deo on my pits, brushed my teeth and got ready for school.

But before I left, I looked at myself in the mirror. The guy staring back was me — but not me. His eyes were real wide, like he was scared of something. And his mouth was a little twisted. But the strangest thing was my hair. There was a white streak in my hair, like I'd been hit by lightning.

*Weird*, I said to myself. *Just weird.*

Amos was watching TV while he waited for me. The news was on — some story about fixing up the city. A big wrecking ball was smashing a building.

"Amos," I said when I saw him. I half expected him to turn around and have no face, or turn into a ghoul.

But Amos just flipped off the TV and smiled at me. "You ready?"

"Yeah, I guess."

"Got your story for Mr. Donkey?"

"I . . . uh . . . . I don't know. Is it due today? I mean, I'm kind of out of it."

"You been sick, Jamal," Amos told me, "but Mr. Donkey won't let you off. You gotta have that story or you're toast, man."

"Well, I started it," I said. "I remember that."

Amos shook his head. "I got my story in early, when you was sick. It was a good one, too."

Amos got up and we both headed to the door. Then we took the stairs down to street level. Amos kept talking about this and that, like nothing had happened. My head kept spinning around. I couldn't make sense of all this.

When we got out on Bendigo Street, I had to get some answers.

"Amos, tell me straight. It feels like my head is full of cotton, you know?"

Amos looked at me. "Well, you've been sick, Jamal. Real sick."

"How sick?"

"Couple of days. It was the usual stuff — high fever, throwing up. At least, that's what your mom told us. All I know is, you were real sick at the clubhouse. You got the sweats, remember that? Just like I got last week. Then Delmar and I took you home. Remember?"

I shook my head. None of this made sense.

"Then I guess you were really out of it, Jamal. Too bad."

We turned the corner to Canal Street. Off to the left were the warehouses. Halfway down the street was our clubhouse . . . and the door . . . and the ghouls.

Amos kept talking as we walked. "You got sick our last day at the clubhouse. Remember? Boy, you broke out into a sweat and started yelling like crazy."

"What about the ghouls?" I asked him.

Amos shook his head. "Those ghouls were in your story, remember? That was a real good story, you know. Too bad there ain't no such thing as ghouls."

"Yeah, too bad," I sighed.

Now we were walking right by "our" warehouse. We were close to the steps that led down to the clubhouse. Up ahead, I could see a guy running toward us. It took a minute to see that it was Delmar. When he reached us, he was out of breath.

"Running late," Delmar panted. "Donkey's gonna kill me."

"No story?" Amos asked.

"Bad story," Delmar replied. "I can't write good, not like Jamal. I mean, Jamal just blinks twice and he's got two hundred words. Me? I gotta think and think to find fifty words . . . and they're bad. I mean, BAAAD."

"So Jamal," Amos asked me. "How'd you finish up your story."

"I . . . uh . . . I don't know." My answer felt lame. But I really didn't know the answer. How did my story end? What was my story about?

"C'mon, Jamal," Delmar said. "We know you got a copy someplace. I mean, a rough draft is okay for us. We don't need the whole fixed up story. But you gotta read it to us before you give it to Mr. Donkey. I mean, how am I gonna learn if you don't show me, right?"

"Hey, I got an idea," Amos said. "How about Jamal reads us the story, like, now. Before school." He looked at his watch. "We got lots of time. The clubhouse is right here."

"Well, I don't know," I said. "I don't know where the story is."

Delmar laughed. "Yeah, like we believe that! You

got it right in your backpack. That's where you always had it. C'mon, Jamal. It won't take no time for you to read it to us. No time at all."

"C'mon, Jamal," Amos joined in.

Delmar had a big smile on his face. But there was something funny about his smile. He had a couple of pointy teeth, way at the back. Funny, I never remembered him with pointy teeth.

Amos was grinning as well. And he had pointy teeth, too.

Amos laughed. "Let's go down to the clubhouse and hear your story, man. You kept us waiting a long time to hear the end of it."

"C'mon," Delmar said, pulling on my arm. "Let's go into the clubhouse."

He was pulling me toward the steps. I felt like I had no strength left. He kept pulling me until we got to the top of the steps, and I saw the door.

At the bottom, it wasn't our clubhouse door. No way. It was the green metal door, with the two pieces making an X, and the bolts. It was the door that held

back the ghouls. Now it was on the outside.

"They gave us a new door while you were sick, Jamal." Amos said. "Pretty nice, eh? But it still has the same lock so we can get inside, no problem."

"C'mon, Jamal," Delmar said. He grabbed my arm and began pulling me toward the clubhouse.

I tried to pull against him. "We're . . . we're gonna be late," I said. My voice was shaky. So were my knees.

"We got lots of time, man," Delmar said. "We just want to hear how your story ends, that's all. Should only take a minute."

Delmar was dragging me. I kept trying to pull free, but Delmar wouldn't let go. His hand felt so cold against my arm. It felt like my arm was freezing in his grip.

"Guys," I pleaded, "it's the door. The door in the wall. Remember?"

"What are you talking about?" Delmar said. "This is the new door to our clubhouse, that's all. How come you're acting so weird?"

I kept trying to pull my arm free from Delmar's grip. "But it's *that* door. You know the one . . . the one with the ghouls behind it."

"Yeah, ri-ight!" Delmar laughed.

"C'mon, Jamal," Amos said. "We've got time. We've got lots of time."

"The three of us always hang out together," Amos said. "But we've been missing you, Jamal. You're the third guy, and we need you. They need you."

Amos opened the door. I could feel freezing air blow out toward us. Inside, it was dark as death, but there were shapes floating in the air.

I was frozen where I stood. Delmar was pulling my arm, but I kept fighting against him.

"Don't be a wuss," Delmar said, still pulling me. "Now get your sorry butt in there."

Amos gave me a push from behind. And that's when I screamed.

If you enjoyed this book, check out this excerpt from Tony Varrato's EDGE novel *Outrage!*

**Outrage!**

**With swollen, bloody hands,** I pulled the door open and walked in. The store was quiet except for the ding when I entered. When I walked past the potato chip rack, I saw the old man who worked there. And he saw me.

Old Riley was one of those guys everybody recognized. He'd been working behind that counter forever. I wasn't sure if Riley was his first name or his last. His face said he was somewhere between seventy and a hundred and seventy, but that tough old guy looked like he could kick some butt. He sure could kick mine right about now.

Riley was filling up the cigarette display behind the counter. He stopped with a carton of smokes still in his hand. I guess he took a look at me and was trying to decide. Should he call the cops or an ambulance?

"Hey, Riley," I mumbled. "It's okay, man." My sore jaw wasn't going to let me say much more. I was trying to let him know I was just here to buy something. There was no need to get out the pepper spray or anything.

I went down the snack aisle and briefly thought about getting a bag of chips. The bag I had for lunch was long gone and my tank was empty. However, just the thought of chewing something made my mouth hurt. I decided to get the frozen Coke and just slurp that until I got home.

I picked the extra large cup and filled it up with the stuff. I grabbed a dome lid and with a little effort I snapped it closed. I had more trouble with the straws. My swollen fingers weren't doing so good with picking up small stuff. I must have dropped about a dozen on the floor. I bent over and had to scoop them up with both hands acting like a clamp.

Then I heard the ding of the door.

I got the straws off the floor, but there was no way they were going back in the little cup. So I dropped them on the counter. *Sorry about that, Riley*, I thought.

I looked toward the counter. The old man was still staring at me. I walked over to the counter, holding the drink between both my nearly useless hands.

I put the drink on the counter and tried to flash Riley a grin. I figured I'd show him my charming side. I had a hunch Riley still wanted to pick up the phone or the pepper spray.

I looked toward the parking lot and saw the car was now empty, but I could hear the thump of the bass. Either the driver had left it on or my head was getting ready to explode.

I reached my right hand into my pocket to get out some money. That's when somebody pushed me. Hard.

I fell toward the counter and bumped my drink. I lurched to catch it before it fell behind and splattered all over the floor.

Maybe it was the hands; maybe it was my messed-up brain head. But I didn't make it. The drink went all over the floor. *Sorry again, Riley.*

Riley jumped back to get out of the way while I was half sprawled on the counter. And then it all happened, in no time.

A guy came around the counter and hit the old man

with a club. Once, twice, and then he stopped. Riley fell to the floor. Then the guy grabbed the bills from the open cash register and headed toward the front door.

I froze for a second. I was still leaning across the counter, feeling stupid. What to do? Help Riley or chase the bad guy?

Easy choice. I was already mad. And the guy had hit an old man.

So I went after the punk. I sprinted with more energy than I thought I had. I got out the door, but the punk had a head start and a running car. All I could do was stand there, wave my arms and yell.

The car was gone.

Did I think to look at the license plate? Of course not. That was one of those things that you yell at the screen when you're watching a hold-up on TV. "Hey, idiot! Get the license plate number!"

Well, I was that idiot. I didn't get the number. I just watched as the dark green car tore down Canal Street. Then I went back in the store to see about Riley.

I walked over to the old man leaning against the wall. Blood was dripping down his head on one side. A big bruise was on the other. He wasn't standing too well.

But he was standing well enough to hold a phone.

"Yeah, I've got one of 'em right here," he said into the phone.

I wanted to say that I wasn't *one of 'em*. But the baseball bat he clutched in his other hand told me to keep my swollen mouth shut.

The sirens were already getting close.

Paul Kropp is the author of many popular novels for young people. His work includes nine novels for young adults, many high-interest novels, and other work for adults and younger children.

Mr. Kropp's best-known novels for young adults, *Moonkid and Liberty* and *Moonkid and Prometheus*, have been translated into many languages and won awards around the world. His two most recent novels are *Running the Bases* and *Homerun*, both published by Doubleday Canada. For more information, see the author's website at www.paulkropp.com.

*For more information on HIP novels:*
High Interest Publishing – Publishers of H·I·P Books
www.hip-books.com